The Good Spy Guide

TRACKING & TRAILING

Ruth Thomson
Judy Hindley

Consultant:
Falcon Travis

Colour Illustration:
Colin King
Black-and-white Illustration:
Liz Graham-Yooll

About this Book

Every successful spy has to be able to follow Enemy Spies, to keep watch on them and learn their secrets without being noticed. He must learn to spot the smallest clues and leave messages that only members of his own Spy Ring can read and understand.

This book is for everyone who wants to be a Good Spy. You can learn how to follow your Quarry through towns or countryside without him knowing you are there; how to move silently by day or night; and how to make and read secret signs. And there are good tricks for fooling Enemy Spies and throwing them off the trail when they are after you.

There are lots of ideas for secret training courses, games to help you practise your spying skills, and puzzles to solve. There are hints on useful equipment to make and how to use it.

First published in 1978 by Usborne Publishing Ltd
20 Garrick Street, London WC2 9BJ, England

Published in Australia by Rigby Ltd
Adelaide, Sydney, Melbourne, Brisbane, Perth

Published in Canada by Hayes Publishing Ltd
Burlington, Ontario

Printed in Belgium by Henri Proost, Turnhout, Belgium.

The Good Spy Guide

TRACKING & TRAILING

Contents

Stalking, Tracking and Shadowing

A Good Spy is able to follow his Quarry—the person he is following—through town or countryside without being noticed. But he has to change his tactics depending on the route taken by the Quarry. Here are some of the main skills you will need to be a Good Spy.

Stalking

In the country, creep after your Quarry as you would follow a wild animal. Move quietly and stay hidden as much as possible. This is called stalking. Your stalking skills will help you to get close enough to watch wild creatures too. This is good practice.

Your clothes should blend into your surroundings and match the main colours of the landscape. Mixtures of colours, such as grey and tan or green and brown, are the best. Choose the ones that go with the type of country where you are stalking your Quarry.

Tracking

If you lose sight of your Quarry, you will have to look for clues to find which way he has gone. Then you can follow them. This is called tracking.

Shadowing

In a town, you must be able to merge with the background so that your Quarry never notices you. You have to follow him at all times without appearing to watch him. This is called shadowing. There are lots of tricks to learn for this.

How to Stalk

When stalking, remember that the crack of a breaking twig or a flicker of movement may give you away. Move silently and smoothly, keeping in the cover of hedges and trees, whenever possible. The next few pages show special walks and crawls for different kinds of cover. Try not to make quick movements, even with your head. Swivel your eyes to look around you. Try to be ready to stop and stay still the moment you see danger.

To walk silently, step very lightly putting each foot down flat, then lifting it carefully clear of the ground. Practise this by walking on dry twigs, stones and gravel.

Remember that animals have a keen sense of smell. If you are stalking an animal, or if the Enemy Spy has a dog, stay downwind so your scent will be blown away from him. If you are upwind, it will blow your scent towards him and you may be discovered.

Look at the picture to get a few more tips.

To check wind direction, wet your finger and hold it up. The colder side faces upwind.

Or toss some dust, dry leaves or bits of grass up into the air. They will blow downwind.

Never stand or walk on the skyline—everyone will be able to see you.

Keep shiny things out of the sun's glare. They may attract attention.

When you stop, keep in the shade, but make sure that your shadow does not give you away.

Checking for Tracks

When searching the ground for tracks, shield your eyes like this, and look towards the sun.

If there is even a small dent in the ground, the shadow made by the sun will make it show up more.

Stalker's Kit

When you go out stalking, always keep your hands free, and only carry the things you think you will really need in your pockets. Try to be prepared for all situations.

Don't carry your kit in a bag or hang things round your neck. They might catch in bushes or fences and make a noise, or drag along the ground and get in your way if you have to crawl any distance. Instead, wear clothes with big pockets and keep everything in them.

Use your front pockets for flat things, such as a map, notebooks and your camouflage headband. Use your back pockets for more bulky things, such as a knife or torch. Then you will not lie on them if you have to crawl along on your stomach.

It is a good idea to take some rations with you in case you get hungry—nuts and raisins are good. Keep them in a small plastic bag with an elastic band twisted round. Below you can see some other things you might find useful.

Camouflage Headband

Cut a band of material long enough to go round your head, and a piece of tape, about 1 metre long.

Pin the tape to the band with safety pins—one at each end and four or five more in between them.

Choose bits of twig, leaves or grass to match your surroundings. Push them between the pins, like this.

You can quickly remove or change your camouflage if you enter a different kind of territory.

Try to wear clothes that blend with your surroundings—dull drab colours are usually best.

They should be old and tough for crawling in, but smooth enough not to catch in spiky bushes.

Stalking Walks and Crawls

When you are stalking an Enemy Spy, you must be very careful to avoid being seen. Make use of things that can hide you—like walls and bushes. These are called 'cover'. Use the stalking approaches shown below when cover is scarce.

The Walk

In good cover, like trees, you can walk upright. But keep your arms still and your hands by your sides.

Feline Crawl

Do this crawl on your hands and knees, keeping your back flat and low. At each step lift your foot just clear of the ground. Do not drag them. Try to keep your head low and do not bob it up and down.

Seal Crawl

Lie flat on your stomach with your legs together and straight, and your toes turned out to keep your heels low. Reach out, pull with your forearms and push with your toes to move forwards.

The Crouch

Near low cover, you may have to crouch to keep your head down. Hold your thighs to help you keep in the crouch position and stay balanced. Do not shuffle. Lift your feet off the ground with each step.

Flat Feline Crawl

Lie slightly sideways, one leg straight and the other bent so the inside of the knee touches the ground. Move by pressing on your forearms and bent knee to slightly raise your body and push it forwards.

Using Cover

The spy in the black hat will easily be seen. The one in the brown hat is making good use of cover. When peering round a wall or tree, remember—one eye is enough. This hides the shape of your head.

Stalking Practice

All these games will help you practise stalking. For the outdoor game shown on the right, you need a good stalking area. Look for a park or garden where there are bushes, dips in the land, long grass or clusters of trees to use as cover. This game will help you learn to use cover, to move quietly, to wait patiently and watchfully, and to spot without being spotted.

Use the indoor games below to train yourself to listen for tiny sounds, to move about silently and stay in one spot without moving.

Clock Hunt

Stalkers should use their ears as much as their eyes, particularly when following a Quarry in woods, dense undergrowth or at night. This game will help you practise doing this.

Any number of people can play. One person hides a clock with a loud tick somewhere in a room, while the others wait outside. These players then have one minute to discover where the clock is hidden, without moving anything in the room.

Steal the Plans

For this game you need at least three players. Put some folded papers under a chair in the middle of the room. One person is the Guard. He sits on the chair blindfolded, with a rolled-up newspaper as a weapon. The others sit down on the floor.

One by one they try to steal the papers without being heard or hit by the Guard. If a player steals the treasure, he becomes the next Guard. If he is hit, he loses his turn.

Beat the Sentries

You need at least four players. Two stand blindfolded either side of an open door. The others, one by one, try to creep from the opposite wall through the door. If a sentry hears a player, he puts out his arm. If the player is touched he goes back to the wall. A player who gets past becomes a sentry.

Hide and Stalk

For this game, you need two players—Stalker and Quarry. If there is a third person, he can take the loser's place after each round. Stalker and Quarry try to spot each other without being spotted.

Choose something like a fallen tree trunk or big stone as your base. The Stalker waits here while the Quarry runs off about 100 metres to hide. He can go further if cover is scarce, but he must stay within earshot. When he has hidden, he shouts 'Ready'! Then the Stalker shouts 'Ready!' and begins to stalk his Quarry.

The first one to spot the other calls his name and says 'You're spotted!' The loser is the Stalker for the next round. To win the game, you have to make three spottings in a row.

When you are the Quarry, think carefully about your tactics. To fool the Stalker, you might try hiding close to base. Wait a bit before you call 'Ready!' to make him think you are further away. Stay quiet until you hear him go past—then creep out behind him.

When you are the Stalker, listen carefully to your Quarry's shout. Try to work out where the sound is coming from, and how far away it is. Try circling round the spot where your Quarry might be hiding to take him by surprise. But remember he can move about as well. Stop from time to time to listen for tell-tale noises.

Training Course

A good stalker can move silently anywhere, even through undergrowth and across stony ground. Here are some ideas for a training course to help you practise.

Set it up somewhere secret with other Good Spies. Take turns to be the Trainer. The Trainer stands with his back to the course while the others, one by one, try to creep up and touch him. Each time he hears a noise, he calls out and the stalker loses a point. See who loses the fewest points while stalking.

Lay planks across some bricks. Scatter stones on them. Each stalker tries to walk them without rattling the stones.

Tie a string between two sticks, like this. Hang pairs of tin lids from it, so low you have to flatten yourself to creep under.

Arrange some tins across the course so that the stalkers must move very carefully to walk past them. Stack the tins or put a few stones in them so they rattle if knocked.

Cover stretches of ground with things that crunch or rustle, like gravel, twigs, dry leaves or newspaper.

1 Clanging Lids

Tie a piece of string round each tin lid. Knot it and hold it in place with bits of sticky tape.

2

Hang the lids on the string, quite close together. Then they will clatter if one of them is touched.

Searchlight

This game tests your skill at moving silently in the dark and listening for noises. You can play it in a garden or field with any number of people. One person is the warder. He carries a torch. The rest are prisoners who try to creep from the start line to the safety line without the warder spotting them. The first prisoner to reach the safety line is the winner, who becomes the next warder. Mark the ground with a start line and a safety line.

When the warder shouts 'Ready!' the prisoners begin creeping to safety. If the warder hears a noise, he points the unlit torch to where he thinks the prisoner is, and shouts 'Halt!' Nobody moves. Then he turns on the torch.

If a prisoner is caught in the torchlight, he must go back ten paces, counting out loud. The warder points the torch upwards to show that everyone else must stay still. When he switches the torch off, the game goes on.

If no one is caught in the torchlight, the warder has made a false challenge and must switch off the torch. If he makes three false challenges, he loses the game and the prisoner nearest to the safety line becomes the warder.

False Challenge

True Challenge

If it is not dark enough, the warder can use a blindfold and look over it after he makes a challenge. Or else the warder can be blindfolded and have an assistant who stands beside him. When the warder makes a challenge, the assistant shouts out 'True' or 'False' but is not allowed to help the warder spot the prisoner. If a prisoner wins, he becomes the assistant, and the assistant becomes the warder. If the warder and assistant win, they swap places for the next game.

Tracking Gadgets

Here are two useful gadgets to help you practise your tracking skills. Work with friends either during the day or at night.

Drag the Whifflepoof by the string. It works well on grass. Make a continuous track or it will be difficult to follow. The tracks show up well at night. If you shine a torch along them, you can see which way they go. They will look darker than the rest of the grass when they are coming towards you and lighter going away.

Use the Tracking Stick like a walking stick. Make a track every few steps on soft, wet ground or on wet sand.

Tracking Stick

You will need
a tin lid with a rim
an old broom handle or thick walking stick
a nail, and a screw about 3 cm long
hammer and screwdriver
pliers

1 **Grip the lid with the pliers and twist them to make a kink in the rim.**

2 **Hammer the nail into the lid to make a hole. Then use it to start a hole in the stick. Get someone to hold the stick while you screw on the lid.**

Whifflepoof

You will need:

a small log
some big nails
a hammer
a piece of cord or thick string, about 3 metres long.

Ask someone to hold the log down firmly on its side for you. Hammer nails all round it, like this. Hammer each one about half-way in.

Hammer two more nails almost right into one end of the log, one on each side. Tie one end of the cord or string round each of these nails.

Covering your Tracks

When you are out in the country, take care not to leave obvious tracks yourself, in case you too are being followed. You should be safe if you stick mainly to hard or stony ground, short grass or fallen leaves. But just in case your pursuer is an experienced tracker, here are some extra tricks that may hold him up and throw him off your track.

Always look ahead and try to plan your route across safe ground—like the carpet of dead leaves in this wood.
Step on bracken or big leaves to avoid making footprints in mud or sand. Remember to pick them up as you go.
If you have to cross a patch of mud, try walking backwards to leave a false trail. (Be sure your tracks are not recognizable—no holes in your shoes)

Using Landmarks

If ever you find yourself coming into territory you do not know—look out for landmarks that will help you to find your way back again. Anything that stands out obviously will do, so long as it cannot move. It must still be there when you want to come back. In towns, use such things as car parks, churches and shops. In the country, look for such things as stiles, gates, farm houses and odd lone trees.

Memorize things so that you recognize them on the way back. Here are some things to look for.

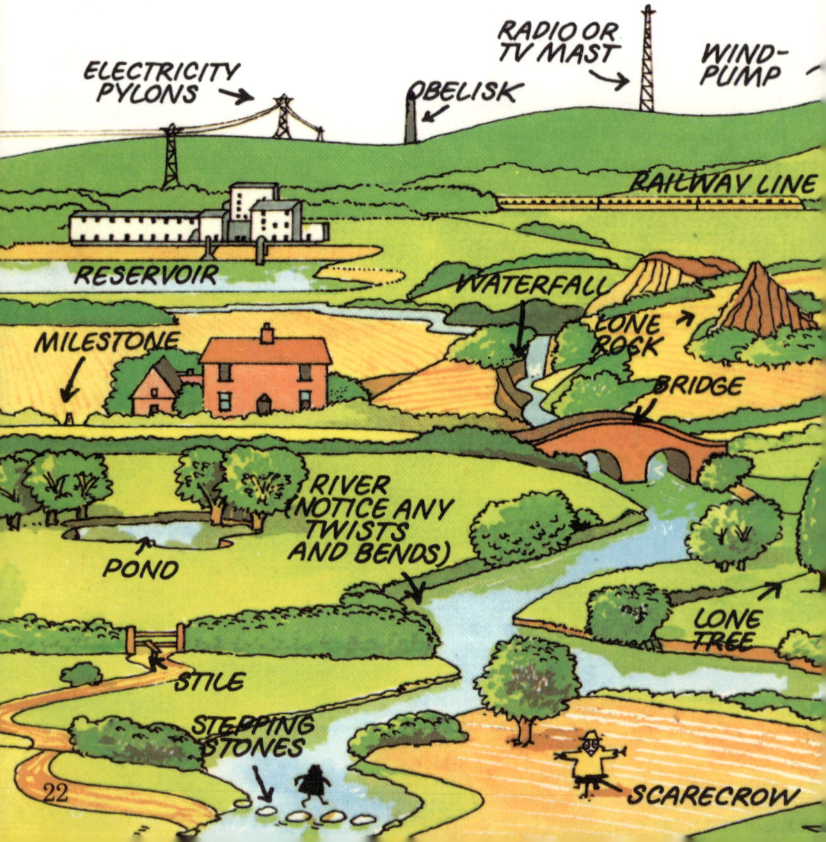

Wherever you are—in the town or country—remember to look back from time to time, especially before you change direction. This will help you to recognize your route on the way back. Remember that things look very different when you are going the other way—you are seeing the other side of them. The things you noted will also be on the other side. Where you turned left on the way out, you will have to turn right coming back.

How to Shadow

When you are shadowing someone, follow them closely enough not to lose contact, but not so closely that you make them suspicious. Glance at them quickly from time to time, but don't stare. Try looking up and down the street as though you are expecting a friend and quickly note where your Quarry is.

Be careful not to stop and start when your Quarry does—he will be sure to notice. When he stops, walk on at the same pace, even if it means you have to pass him. Then make some excuse to stop and wait until he comes past, then you can begin to follow again.

Keep a sharp look-out when your Quarry gets close to a corner.

If you are not looking, he may be out of sight before you realise.

Good Spies learn to use their eyes without moving their heads—like this.

If you can see your Quarry's reflection, it means he can see yours.

Be prepared before you go out, with lots of different excuses for stopping. You must take care to vary your tactics because your Quarry will be sure to notice if you use the same excuse several times. Look at things in shop windows or ask someone for directions.

If there is a lot of traffic, walk to the edge of the pavement, and pretend to be waiting to cross the road. When your Quarry moves on, don't follow him straightaway, but keep him in sight. If you suspect he is watching you in the reflection of a window, try the window check shown below.

When you hurry after him, slow down again before you reach the corner.

Saunter round it casually. If he really is a spy, he may be bluffing too.

To see if he is watching you, move so he cannot see your reflection.

If he is suspicious, he will move to try and catch sight of you again.

Shadow's Kit

When you are out on a secret mission, trailing a Quarry, it will be vital that he does not suspect what you are doing. It is best to wear ordinary clothes so you won't be noticed in a crowd. But in case you are spotted, it is a good idea to have a quick disguise kit to change into. Keep it in a carrier bag which you can put in your pocket afterwards.

Try carrying a different coloured jersey or jacket with you, or putting on a hat or scarf so that you look a different shape from a distance. Remember to wear soft-soled shoes so that you can walk quietly and also run fast if you need to.

It may be useful to carry a notebook to keep a record of your Quarry's movements and any suspicious activities. Or you may want to take down information such as car numbers, train times or descriptions. If you have a street map, you can mark the route your suspect takes, follow him without getting lost, and see where you can take short cuts.

If you think your Quarry has spotted you . . . **make a quick obvious change in your looks.**

If you want an excuse to stop and spy, when your Quarry stops, carry a newspaper, map or comic.

But be very careful. Lower it just enough to peep over the top, without staring obviously.

Use this double- mirror to spy over your shoulder. Move it carefully to get the view you want.

You can camouflage it as a diary, as shown below. Or just slip it inside a book or comic.

Tape two small handbag mirrors together on one side, like this. Make sure you can open and close them easily.

Tear all but the first and last pages from an old diary. Slip the mirror between them to make the Spyscope.

Shaking off a Tail

Remember that Enemy Spies might try to shadow you too, so try to think about what they might do, and how you could avoid being followed or 'tailed'. Follow the spy in the brown hat round the picture, and see how he shakes off the Enemy Spies, who are wearing blue coats.

Use reflections in shop or car windows to see if you are being followed.

To cross a street where you might be spotted, wait until you can be shielded by other people.

Planning a Route

If you want to keep your destination secret, it is very important to plan your route carefully. Here are some useful tips:

1. Do not approach your destination by a direct route. Use a zig-zag or roundabout path.
2. Vary your route—do not go the same way every time.
3. Do not walk fast—this may alert the Enemy Stroll along looking at buildings and read notices as if you are out for a walk.

Look for side streets with turnings in easy reach. Dodge in when your tail's view is blocked.

Once you are out of sight of your tail, avoid long stretches of street until you are safely clear.

Turn-about Trick

Stop and gaze into a shop window. Often your tail will stop too. Then turn and walk towards him.

If your tail walks away, you can disappear down a side street while his back is turned.

Catch the Spy

This is an outdoors spying game for two teams. One team (the Spy Ring) is made up of Couriers plus a Spy. The other team are Spycatchers.

Each Courier tries to deliver a message (a rolled-up newspaper) to the Spy at a secret Rendezvous, and then protect him as he delivers the message to a Control spot.

Each Spycatcher tries to discover the secret Rendezvous by shadowing one of the Couriers. He then tries to arrest the Spy as the Spy carries all the messages to a Control spot.

How to play the game:

1. Together, the teams choose starting points and two Controls as on the map. Chalk a large circle on the ground at each Control.
2. The Spy Ring meet secretly to choose a Rendezvous, and the Spy has a 3-minute start to get there. He chalks another circle at the Rendezvous. (The Spy is always safe when standing inside a chalk circle.)
3. Then the Couriers wave to the Spycatchers and make for the Rendezvous.
4. The Spycatchers follow as secretly as possible, so as not to be arrested (touched by a Courier). If arrested, they must freeze until the Courier is out of sight.
5. The Spy stays at the Rendezvous until he has all the messages. (The Couriers can scout around to see which Control might be safest.) Then the Spy makes for one of the Controls, guarded by the Couriers.
6. If the Spy is arrested with his messages, the Spycatchers have won. If he reaches a Control safely, the Spy Ring has won.

This street map shows how to set up the game. The distances between the Controls and the Starting Point should be about 500 paces.

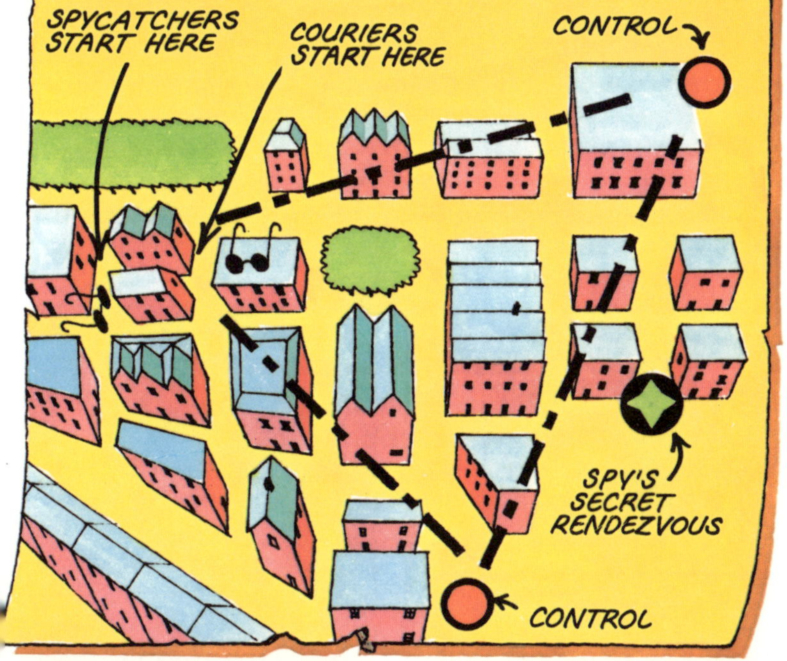

SPYCATCHERS START HERE

COURIERS START HERE

CONTROL

SPY'S SECRET RENDEZVOUS

CONTROL

A Courier cannot be arrested. He can arrest a Spycatcher by touching him.

To arrest the Spy, a Spycatcher must touch him before being touched by a Courier.

Trail Signs

Here are some special signs you can use to show a contact where you have gone. They may be useful if you have left your hide-out to stalk Enemy Spies.

Make them with twigs, stones or deep scratches in the ground. They should be just big enough for a careful observer to see them. Put them in sheltered places or at the side of your path so they will not be disturbed by other walkers. Make sure that you are not watched while you are laying the trail.

Study the pictures carefully. Then turn the page and see if you can remember what the signs mean.

Trail Tips

Remember—a good trail layer only leaves signs where they are really needed. Use them to show a change of direction, or where there is a choice of paths. If there is no path, leave signs about every 20 paces. Try to follow the trail in this picture without turning back to check the signs.

LEAVE A SIGN TO MARK ANY CHANGE OF DIRECTION.
TRY TO PUT THE SIGNS AT THE SIDE OF YOUR PATH, OR IN A SHELTERED PLACE, SO THEY WILL NOT BE DISTURBED.
DON'T LEAVE MORE SIGNS THAN ARE NEEDED. IT WASTES TIME AND ATTRACTS THE WRONG KIND OF ATTENTION.
REMEMBER—'ONE PACE' MEANS ONE ORDINARY WALKING STEP. MAKE SURE ALL YOUR FOLLOWERS KNOW THIS.

On the Trail

Test how well you know the trail signs shown on the last pages. Follow the 'ground signs' here until you come to a 'message hidden' sign. It will give you a clue to where to pick up the trail again. You will only understand it if you have followed the route correctly from the start. It starts at a place for learners . . . Turn to the last page to check what you find.

NORTH STAR INN
JOLLY DRUID'S INN
FOX INN
DRUID'S POND
AT POST OFFICE CROSSROADS GO IN OPPOSITE DIRECTION TO THAT IN TWINKLY NAME.
DRUID'S GROVE
POST OFFICE
CONTINUE TRAIL AT CHURCH NEAR POND- NOT 'OTHER' CHURCH OR 'OTHER POND.
LONG LAKE
N
W
E
S

Indian Signs

Use these signs for messages when you are on the trail. Chalk them on stones or scratch them on dry earth. They are based on the picture-writing used by Sioux Indians, who scratched messages on dried animal skins and pieces of tree bark.

Time of Day

MORNING NOON EVENING

Weather and Landscape

GRASS

Camp

War
FIGHT(WAR)
PRISONER
ENEMY (BEAR)
DEFEATED ENEMY (DEAD BEAR)
Describing People
MAN
WOMAN
FRIENDS (BROTHERS)
SAME GANG (SAME TRIBE)
Describing Actions
HUNGRY
EAT
FLEE
TALK
TALK
SEE
HEAR
STRONG
Other Useful Signs
NEAR OR NEARBY
NO OR NOT (DEATH)
HOUSE
TOWN
BAD
COME OR BRING
REACH OR REACHED
PEACE

Indian Messages

These messages were left for you by your Contact. Can you work out what they mean? Use your imagination and a bit of guess work. Don't 'read' the signs one by one, like words in a sentence. Check your answers on the last page.

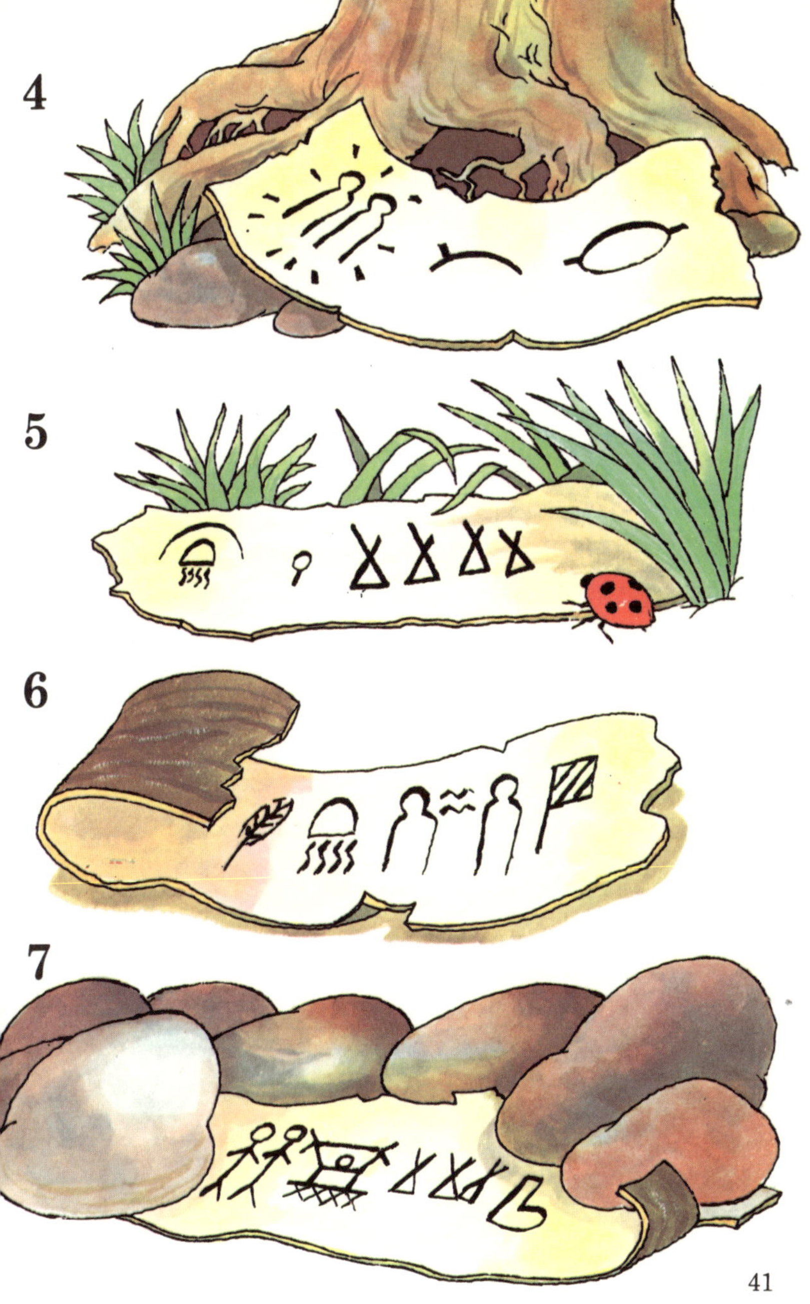
4
5
6
7

Secret Ground Signs

You can use these secret ground signs to pass messages to your Contacts which only you and they will understand. First you must all agree what each of the signs means, and where each of you will leave your messages. You can also use them when you are laying a trail.

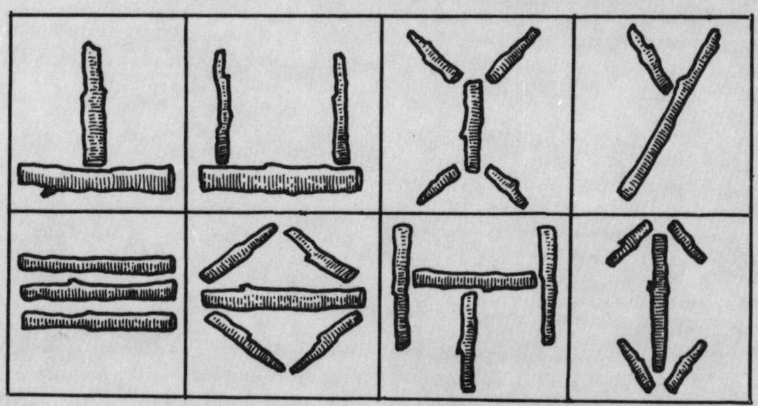

Make signs like these with bits of stick to tell your Contact where to collect messages. They could say 'Behind the gate' or 'Under the mat'.

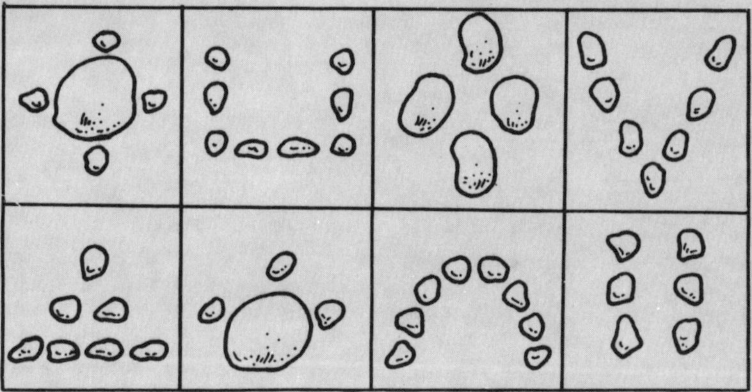

Here are some signs made with stones. Use them to leave warning messages such as 'Avoid the Hideout' or 'You are being followed.'

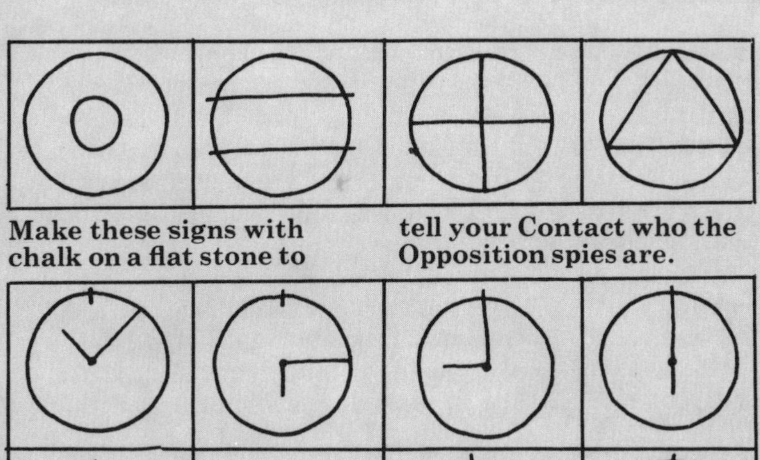

Make these signs with chalk on a flat stone to tell your Contact who the Opposition spies are.

Use signs like these to tell your Contact when to meet you. Draw a circle on a post, wall or flat stone, and add a small mark to show 12 o'clock. Then put in the hands to show the time.

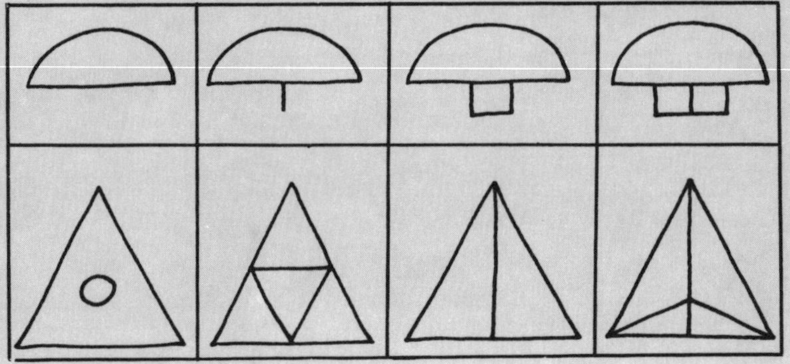

Use these to tell your Contact where to meet you. By using two signs you could leave a message such as 'Meet me behind the church at six.'

Man-Made Tracks

A good tracker should study footprints and tyre marks when he is on a trail. If they have been made by his Quarry, they may give useful clues about him—such as how fast he is moving and which way he is heading. They may also show whether the Quarry has stopped or met anyone else on the way.

Tracks show up best in soft ground. Try looking for them in loose earth, mud, snow or in firm sand. You should look for clearly marked, fresh footprints and tyre marks. If you find dry, cracked tracks, or if there are puddles in footprints, the tracks are old and were probably not made by your Quarry.

Remember to look out for obvious clues when you are out trailing. Does your Quarry have a dog with him, or is he using a walking stick? He might be carrying something heavy, or be limping, which would slow him down. Check the size of any footprints you find to see if they could have been made by your Quarry. Look at the next page for some more clues.

The front wheel of a cycle makes a loopy track as the cyclist turns it from side to side to keep his balance. As he goes faster he turns it less, so the loops are flatter. The narrow end of the loops point in the direction where the cyclist is heading.

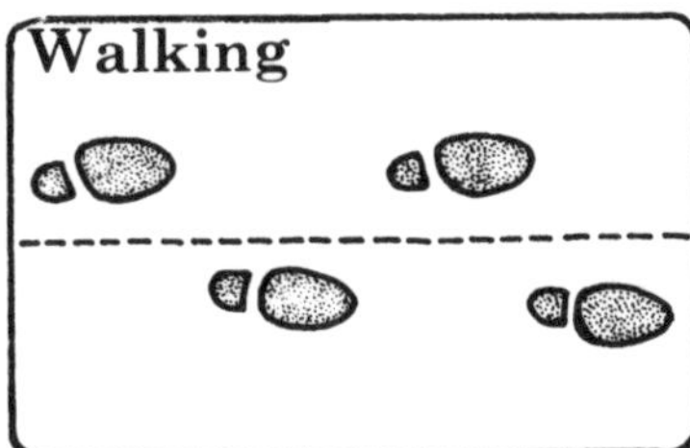

If your Quarry is walking slowly, you will see whole footprints. Both toe and heel will show.

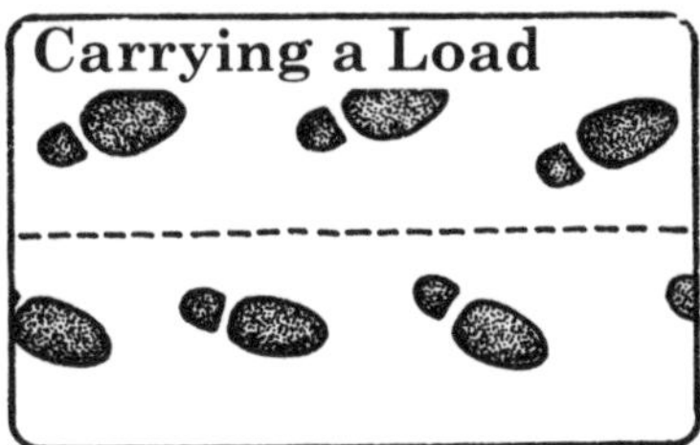

If he is carrying a heavy load, the footprints will be deeper and spread further apart.

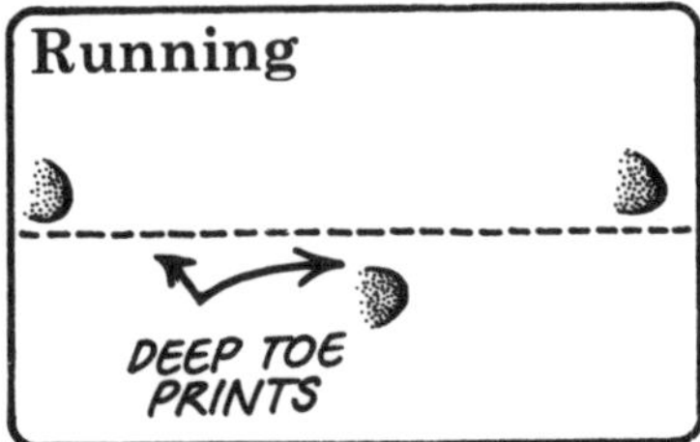

The prints of a running Quarry will be in a line. If he is running fast, only toe prints will show.

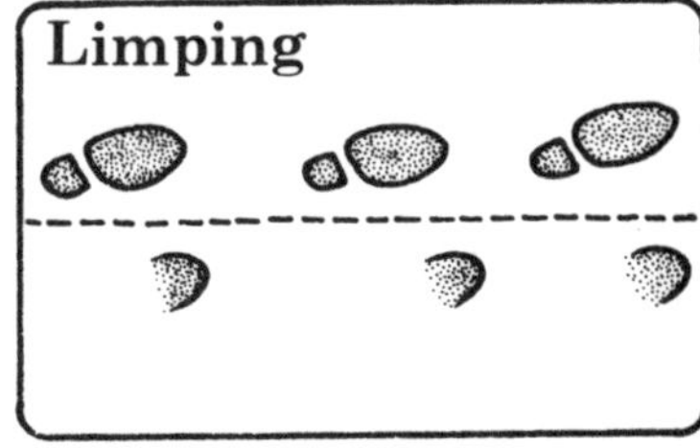

If he is limping, one footprint will be deep, and you will only be able to see part of the other.

You can tell which of two tracks is more recent because the newer track will cut across the older one. The stone kicked backwards and the puddle splashed forwards show the direction that the car which left the tracks was travelling in.

Track Puzzle

The tracks in the snow tell a whole story. This is Station Road, half-an-hour after the accident which later made headline news in the local newspaper. Can you work out what happened? Check your answers on the last page.

Daily News
MAN WITH DOG IN
HIT-AND-RUN ACCIDENT

Tracking Signs

There are lots of signs you can look out for when you are on a trail. The clues will vary according to the sort of ground you are walking on and if it is wet or dry.

A good tracker will make a note of these things so that he can look for signs in the right places. When you are trailing a Quarry, look around you very carefully. A small sign might be a big clue. It is a good idea to practise observing things whenever you are out in the country or a park. Try stopping every now and again to listen for noises. Remember that animals and birds can show that someone is moving about.

In woodlands, look at the ground. If someone has walked through dead leaves recently he may have made a trail. The leaves that have been turned over will be damp and darker than top ones.

Look for trails in long grass. If someone has walked through it, you will be able to see where the stems have been pushed apart. If he sat down, the grass will be flat and the stems crushed.

Look for trails, like this, in soft sand. There will be small hollows where someone has walked instead of footprints.

Look at the grass under any object you find. If it is pale or yellow the object has been there for quite a few days.

On dry, dusty ground look for small stones which have been kicked about. There may be scuff marks from a Quarry's shoes.

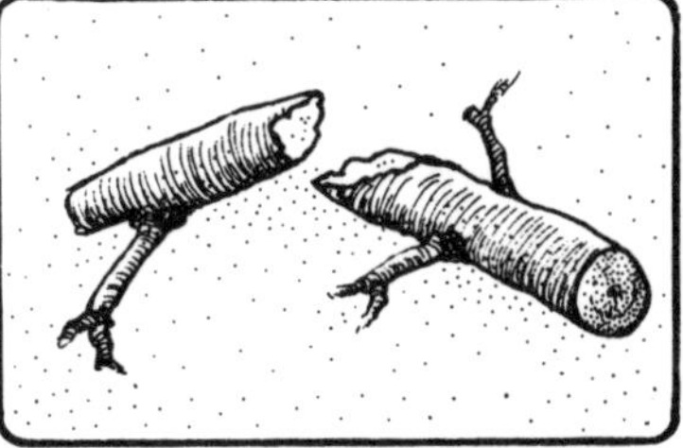

Twigs are sometimes bent or broken by someone walking on them. If a break is new, the wood will be bright and pale.

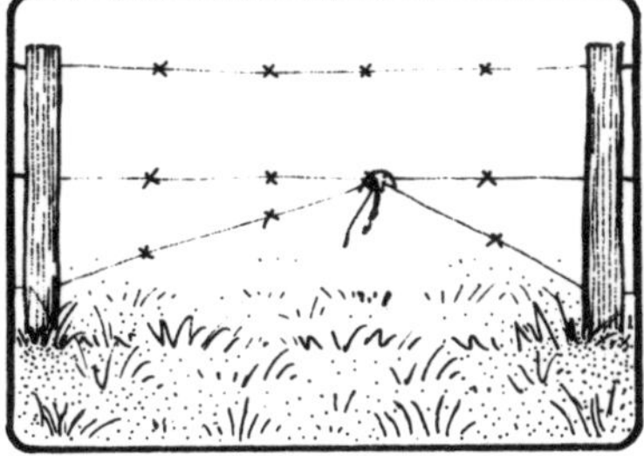

Someone crawling under a fence has hooked up the wire. There is a thread of torn clothes and the grass is flattened underneath.

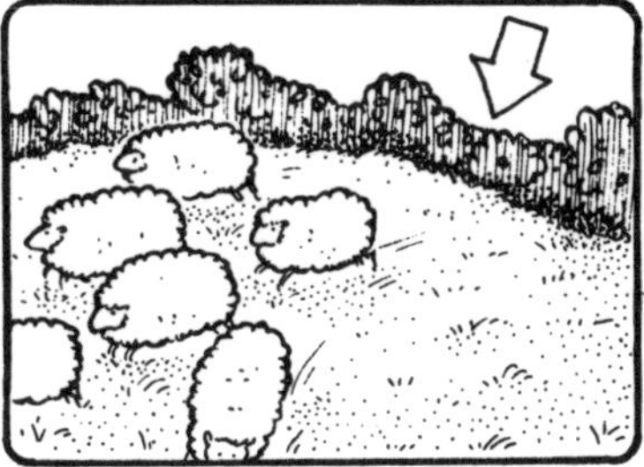

Animals, such as sheep, running as if frightened, may mean someone is there. He may be creeping along the hedge.

Picking up a Trail

When you are following a trail you may lose sight of your Quarry, particularly in woods or where the path divides. If you do, try to find it again as quickly as you can First look around you for obvious signs. You may see birds suddenly flying up ahead as if they have been frightened or animals running away.

Listen hard for noises which might give you a clue, such as the rustle of someone walking through dry leaves. Or your Quarry may sing or whistle, not knowing he is being followed.

Next look at the ground around you very carefully. If you find a fresh footprint, note which way it is pointing and go in that direction. If you do not find footprints, try walking round your starting point in a small circle, searching hard. Walk in a bigger and bigger circle until you find a clue.

The picture below shows the trail left by a Quarry who is now out of sight. See if you can spot the clues which show which path he has taken. Check your answers on the last page.

Hoof Prints

Whenever you are out in the country or in any open ground, practise your stalking and tracking skills. This will help you to notice small signs when you are on the trail of a Quarry and he is out of sight.

Look carefully at patches of wet earth, wet sand or snow where prints show up well. You can also see them on grass or leaves after rain.

Horses and Cows

The hoofs of horses, wild ponies and cows are about the same size but have different shapes. If a horse is shod, you will see only the track of its shoes (a). If it is unshod, you will see an almost round track with a dent at the back (b).

If a horse is going fast, you may see scuff marks in front of each hoof mark. Cows have split hoofs (c).

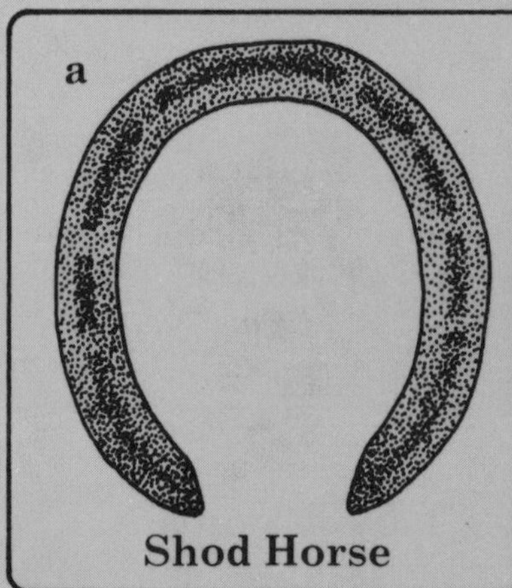

Shod Horse

Deer, Sheep and Goats

Deer, sheep and goats also have split hoofs, like cows, but they are much smaller. When you find small hoof prints, like these, look for other clues. If they have been made by sheep, look for bits of wool caught on hedges or wire fences. Deer sometimes nibble the bark off trees a few inches from the ground.

Red Deer

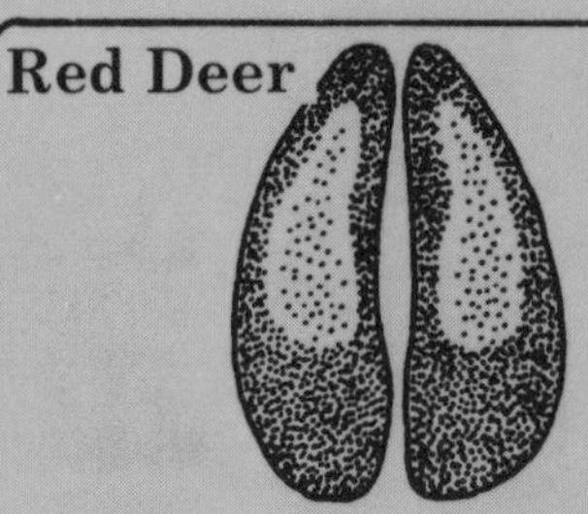

These hoofs curve towards one another at the tip. You may see a print of the round pads at the back.

Learn to recognize animal prints and to see which way the animals went. Practise stalking very quietly to see how close you can get to an animal before it is frightened away. This is also a good test of your camouflage clothes.

Remember that some animals can be dangerous if you go too near. Keep away from any animals that have young babies with them.

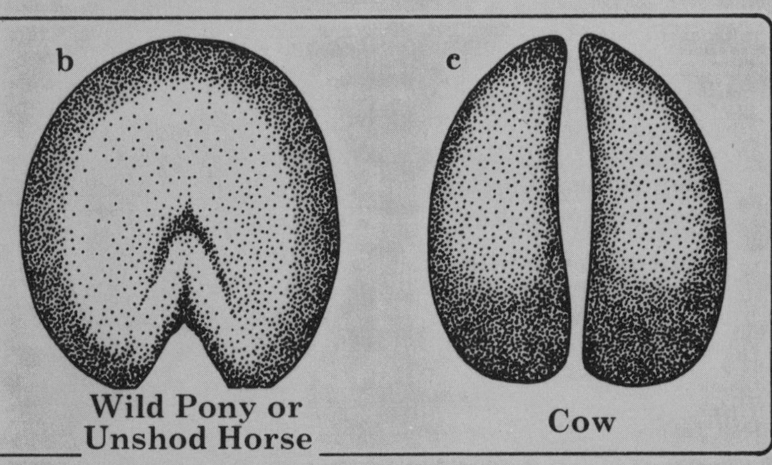

Wild Pony or Unshod Horse

Cow

Sheep

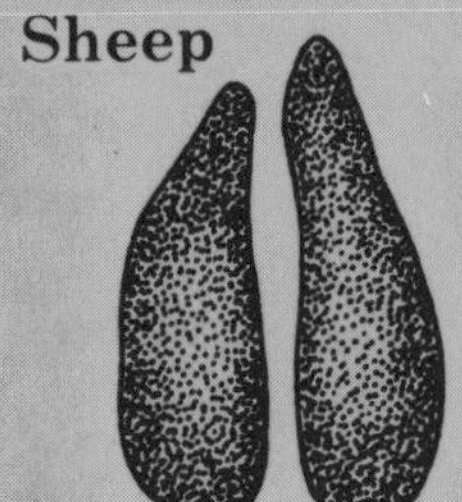

Sheeps' hoofs are wider at the back than at the front and have rounded tips.

Goat

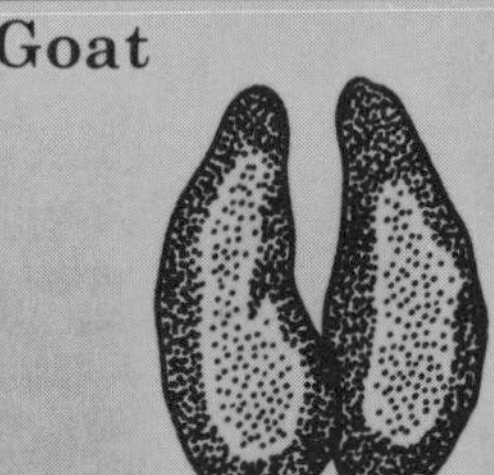

Goats' hoofs have rounded tips and curve in towards one another.

Paw Prints

A good tracker learns to recognize all the footprints he sees. It is useful to know if your Quarry has a dog with him. and if it is a big dog. You may have to change your tracking methods if it is. Remember that dogs have a very keen sense of smell and may know you are there. even if it and your Quarry cannot see you.

Dogs sometimes run out and bark at strangers or follow them for a while. If this has happened to your Quarry as he tried to sneak past a house. the dog tracks might give him away—although your Quarry was careful not to leave any tracks himself.

The prints made by dogs and cats often look alike but a dog's prints are usually larger. It is useful if you learn to tell them apart. Look at the prints on the next page to see how they are different. It is a good idea to watch a dog or cat crossing some mud or sand. Then look at the trail it has made. Examine the tracks carefully and see how they change when the cat or dog walks slowly and then runs.

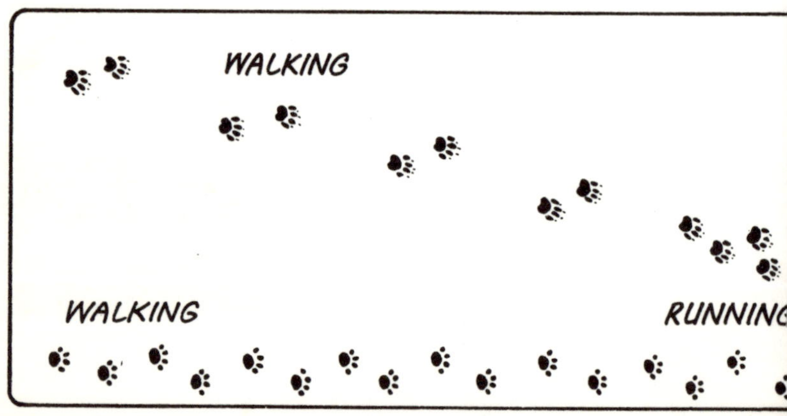

Dog Print

Dog prints usually look like this, although they may be bigger or smaller. The pad is shaped like a triangle and there are four toe prints. The pad mark is larger than the toes. There is one longish claw mark at the end of each toe. The claws may be worn down.

Cat Print

You can tell the difference between dog and cat tracks because cat tracks are small and do not have claw marks. The claw marks show only if the cat has landed on the ground after jumping from a height. When cats walk, they draw their claws into the end of their toes.

Bird Tracks

If you live in a town where you are not likely to see the footprints of horses and wild animals, look for bird prints instead. This is good tracking practise and you can pick up quite a lot of clues about birds.

Look for bird prints in gardens, parks, on the edges of lakes and ponds, in zoos and wild life parks. Birds which live mostly in bushes and trees are usually small and light. They have pointed claws and a long back toe to grip branches. They often hop along the ground, looking for food.

Larger, heavier birds, such as partridges and pheasants, have short, strong feet for running along the ground. Their tracks run almost in a straight line or in a zigzag. Look for wading bird tracks in sand or mud on the banks of rivers or ponds. You might see the webbed feet of swimming birds too.

On the next page is a Track Trap to make. Birds walking across it will leave clear footprints.

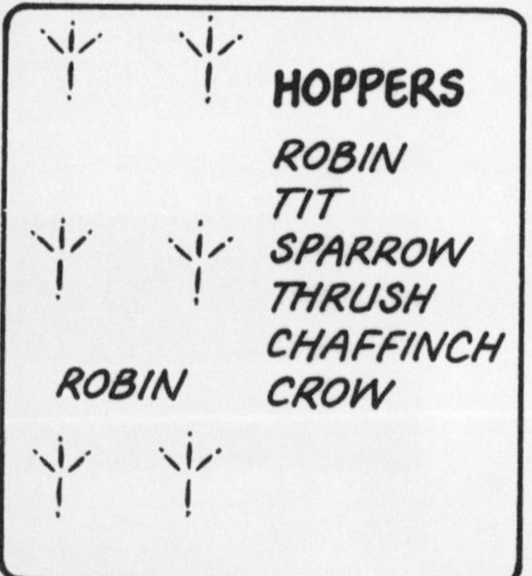

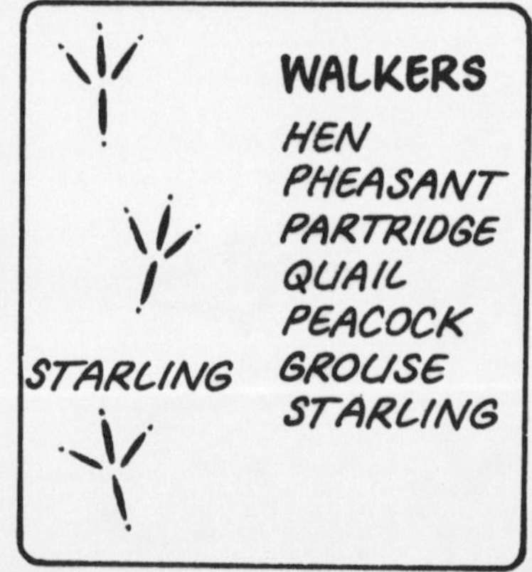

TRACK TRAP

YOU WILL NEED:

- SHEET OF BROWN PAPER
- SOME FLOUR
- BREAD CRUMBS

ON A DRY DAY LAY THE BROWN PAPER ON THE GROUND AND SPREAD FLOUR ROUND THE EDGES

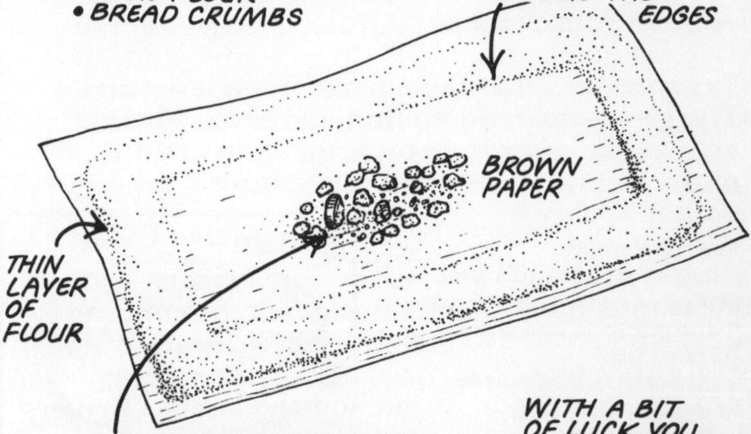

BROWN PAPER

THIN LAYER OF FLOUR

PUT SOME BREADCRUMBS IN THE MIDDLE OF THE SHEET. LEAVE THEM OVERNIGHT.

WITH A BIT OF LUCK YOU SHOULD FIND SOME TRACKS ON THE PAPER NEXT MORNING.

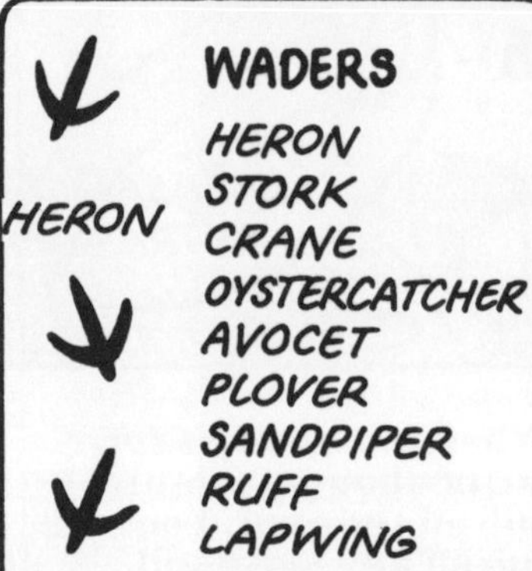

Making Plaster Casts

A collection of plaster casts is very useful for tracking practice. Casts which are a copy of the foot or paw which made the track are called negative. Casts which copy the track itself are called positive. Use negative casts to make trails for tracking practice, and positive ones to help you recognize tracks.

Try to make casts from clear, complete tracks. The ground should be firm and level. Make a note of the animal or bird, the date and the place. Scratch this on the cast later.

You will need
a bag of plaster of Paris
strips of card about 6 cm long and 12 cm wide
paper clips
a jar half-full of water
teaspoon and old toothbrush
vaseline or grease
newspaper for wrapping the finished casts
pieces of string

1 Negative Casts

Grease the inside of a card strip, so that the plaster will not stick. Fix it round the track, using a paper clip.

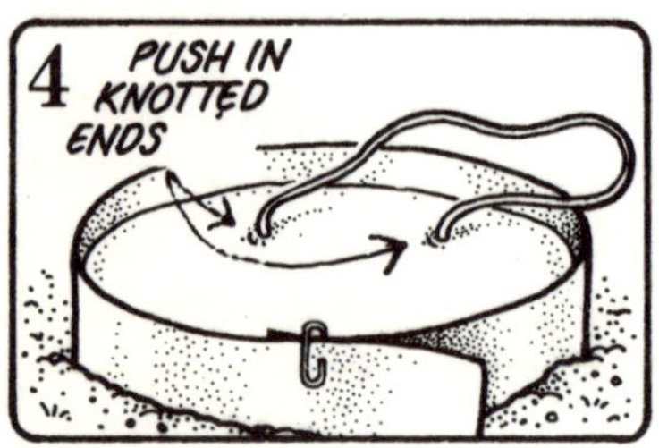

Push a bit of string deep down into one side of the cast before it hardens. You will be able to hang it up by this later on.

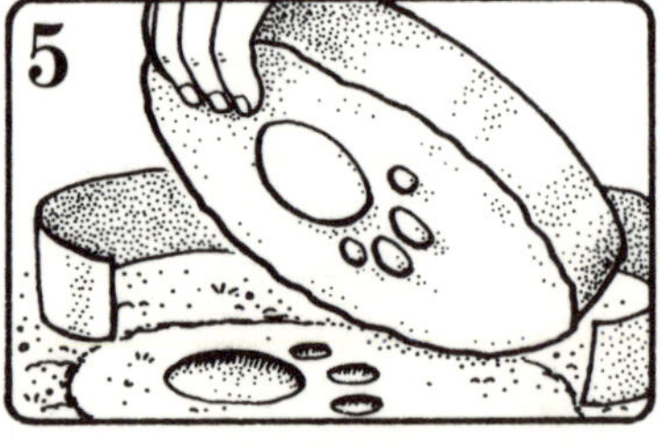

When the cast has set, (after about 20 minutes), pull off the card. You can rub off any loose soil with an old toothbrush.

Using Plaster of Paris

You can buy plaster of Paris in hardware stores. Here are some tips:

Pour the plaster into the water, stirring with your free hand. A pinch of salt makes it dry faster. Don't add the water to the plaster, as it will go lumpy.

Touch it to see if it has set. At first it will be warm. But it will dry as it cools.

Plaster sets quickly. Never pour it down a drain, or it will block it up. Pour left-over plaster on to newspaper, then throw it out. Rinse the spoon and jar as soon as you have finished.

Slowly pour plaster into a small jar of water, stirring all the time, until it is smooth and runny like thick cream.

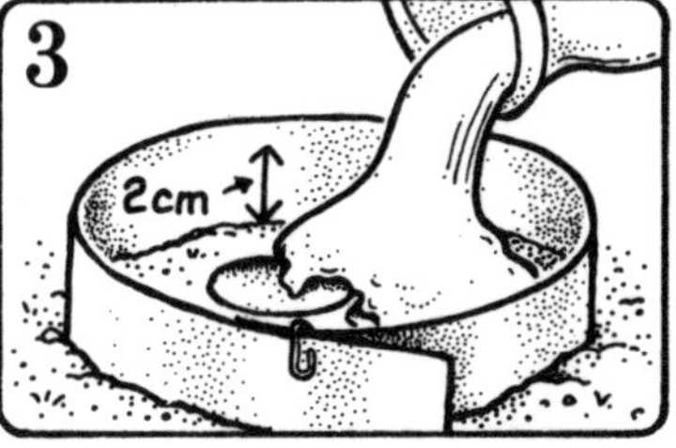

Before the mixture dries, pour it steadily over the track. Pour from one side until the cast is about 2 cm thick.

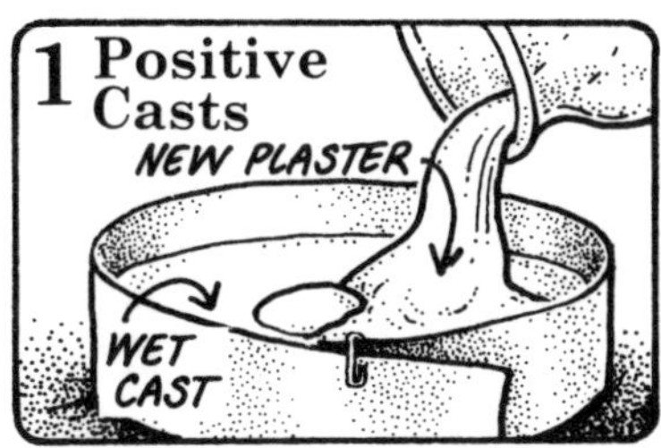

Turn the negative cast over inside the card and smear the top with soapy water. Now pour on the next layer of wet plaster.

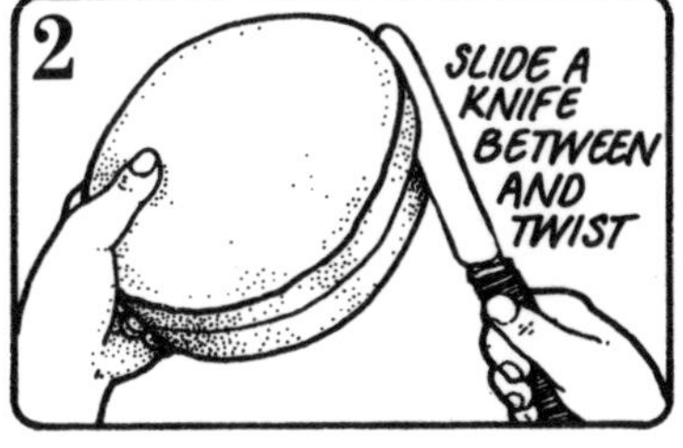

When this plaster has set and is hard, pull off the card wall. Gently separate the two casts with a knife, like this.

Useful Measurements

A Good Spy uses his own body measurements to work out the size of such things as footprints, distances and the height of his Quarry.

Take your own measurements with a ruler or tape measure. Remember them or write them on this chart. You will have to change them every six months if you are still growing.

By knowing the length of your own shoes, you can guess how tall your Quarry is by the size of his footprints. Short people usually have small feet. Tall people have big feet. Measure the length of your stride and use it to guess how tall your Quarry is. Tall people usually walk with big strides. Short people and women take little steps.

You can also use the length of your stride to work out distances. Count your steps as you walk along. Then multiply the number of steps by the size of your stride to get the distance. Use the other measurements to work out the heights of people and things.

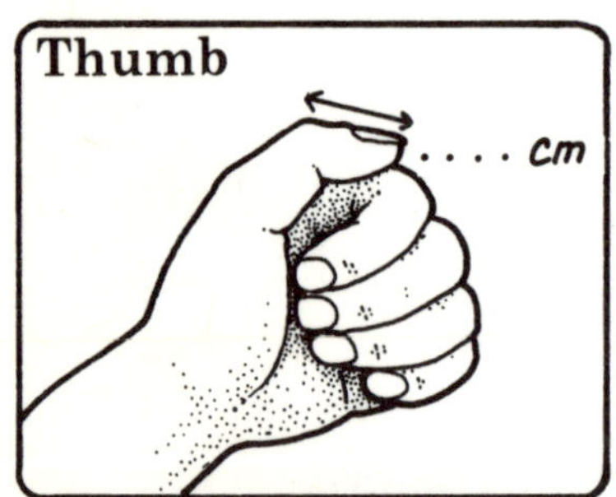

Hold your thumb like this to measure from the tip to the joint accurately.

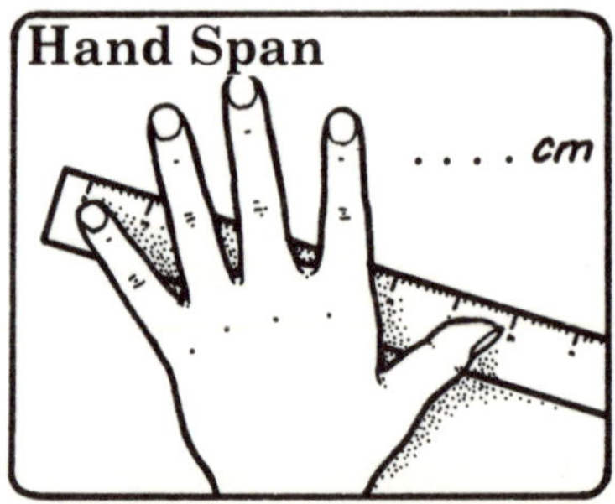

Spread your hand out as wide as you can like this. Lay it across a flat ruler.

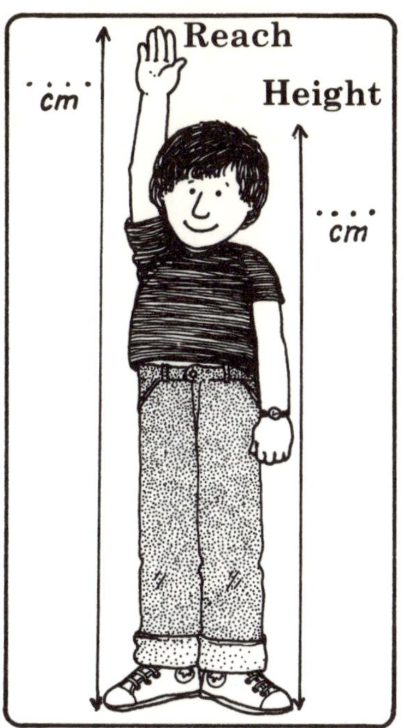

Stand up straight with your back against a wall and your heels together to measure your height.

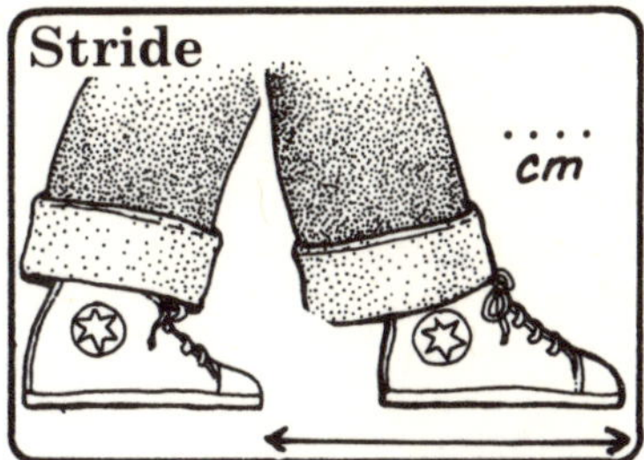

Take an ordinary stride and measure the distance from the toe of one shoe to the toe of the other.

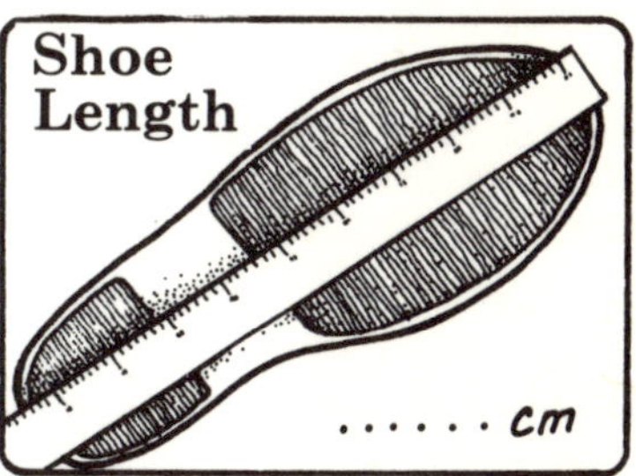

Measure the exact length of one of your feet from heel to toe.

Measure your outstretched arms finger tip to finger tip (a). Then cut a piece of string one metre long and see how far across your body it reaches (b).

Spy Language

Agent—A spy.

Briefing—A meeting when spies are given information and instructions about an assignment.

Camouflage—Clothes worn by a spy which blend into the background so he is not noticed by his Quarry.

Classified Information—Information that is so secret that only specially chosen people are allowed to know about it.

Contact—A member of a Spy Ring who works with other members.

Courier—A spy who carries and delivers secret messages, information or instructions to other spies.

Cover—Anything, such as buildings or bushes, which a spy hides behind.

Headquarters (H.Q.)—The place, perhaps secret, a spy ring operates from.

Imposter—A spy who is disguised to look like, and pretends to be, another person.

Master Spy—The head of a Spy Ring who directs its operations.

The Opposition—The enemy spies.

Quarry—Someone who is secretly stalked, tracked or shadowed.

Rendezvous—A secret place where spies arrange to meet.

Set-up—A trap to catch an Enemy Spy.

Shadowing—Following and keeping watch on a Quarry in a town without him knowing.

Spy Ring—A group of spies who work together secretly.

Stalking—Following a Quarry secretly by moving quietly through the countryside and staying hidden.

Surveillance—Keeping watch secretly on an Enemy Spy, or on a building which Enemy Spies use as their H.Q. or as a Rendezvous.

Suspect—A person suspected of being a spy.

Tail—A spy who shadows another spy.

Tracking—Following the tracks left by a Quarry when he is out of sight.

Trail—The tracks left accidentally by a Quarry, or the clues and messages left by a member of a Spy Ring for his Contact to follow.

Trainer—An expert spy who teaches other spies useful skills.

Undercover Agent—A spy operating in disguise in enemy territory.

Answers

Answers to Trail Signs Puzzle on pages 32 and 33

The place for learners is, of course, the school. Follow the arrows to the first message. The inn with the twinkly name is the North Star. Follow the arrows. At the Post Office crossroads, go in the opposite direction to the north. To do this, look at the sign at the bottom right of the right-hand page and go south. Follow the arrows. Go to the other church. Follow the arrows. Go to the other pond—Druid's Pond. The sign there says 'your Contact has gone home'.

Answers to Indian Messages on pages 40 and 41

1. Hide in the forest near the river.
2. No night meeting.
3. Bring rations to the camp fire in the evening.
4. Meeting in the morning by the lake.
5. Enemy hidden near camp.
6. Leaders of the enemy talk together about peace.
7. People have discovered our hideout—flee.

Answers to Track Puzzle on pages 46 and 47

The tracks coming from the right are those of a man walking his dog. The dog sees a cat at the top right and dashes off, dragging its lead. The cat climbs a tree and the dog waits below. Meanwhile, the man darts into the road after the dog, is hit by a motorcyclist. Motorcyclist rides off. Man at top left runs to help injured man to a chair brought by a lady from the house, middle top. Man coming from bottom left runs to telephone box to call ambulance. Ambulance arrives. Injured man is helped into it by first helper, who climbs in with him. Both drive off in ambulance. And that's the story.

Answers to the Picking Up a Trail Puzzle on pages 50 and 51.

The Quarry has climbed over the gate and taken the path to the right of the clearing. There are five clues:

1. Footprint just in front of gate.
2. Mud scraped on bars of gate.
3. Birds flying up beyond the bushes on the right side of the clearing.
4. Cows staring along the right-hand path.
5. Birds and rabbits on the centre and left-hand paths feeding quietly.